Explore

Christy Goerzen

Orca currents

ORCA BOOK PUBLISHERS

Library and Archives Canada Cataloguing in Publication

Goerzen, Christy, 1975-

Explore / written by Christy Goerzen.

(Orca currents)

ISBN 978-1-55469-120-3 (bound).--ISBN 978-1-55469-119-7 (pbk.)

I. Title. II. Series.

PS8613.O38E96 2009   jC813'.6   C2008-907415-7

Summary: Mike explores the world of outdoor recreation and discovers
a new side of himself.

First published in the United States, 2009
Library of Congress Control Number: 2008941142

Orca Book Publishers gratefully acknowledges the support for its publishing
programs provided by the following agencies: the Government of Canada
through the Book Publishing Industry Development Program and the
Canada Council for the Arts, and the Province of British Columbia
through the BC Arts Council and the Book Publishing Tax Credit.

Cover design by Teresa Bubela
Cover photography by Dreamstime
Author photo by Kimberly Malysheff

Orca Book Publishers   Orca Book Publishers
PO Box 5626, Station B   PO Box 468
Victoria, BC Canada   Custer, WA USA
V8R 6S4   98240-0468

www.orcabook.com
Printed and bound in Canada.
Printed on 100% PCW recycled paper.

12 11 10 09 • 4 3 2 1

For Joshua, with truckloads of love

chapter one

I was surrounded by a sea of Gore-Tex, wooly toques and rosy cheeks. *Granolas.* That's what my buddy Cam calls them. A girl near me with red hair in long braids was eating something out of a pottery bowl. It looked like orange sections with yogurt and oat flakes. *Holy crap,* I thought, *Granolas even* eat *granola.*

I sat at the back of the room in my old hoodie and jeans I hadn't washed in months, my face still creased from the bedsheets.

I felt out of place. There were about twenty kids in the room, all looking pretty bright-eyed for seven thirty in the morning. There was no way I'd be here if Officer Lardface hadn't parked outside my bedroom window and honked the horn, over and over again, until I stumbled outside.

When I first arrived, a guy and a woman in matching fleece jackets were stacking papers and talking quietly. I stood in the doorway, not sure what to do. The guy snapped his head up immediately, a massive grin on his leathery face. Between the two of them, they'd probably had more years in the sun than most California surfers.

"Heyyyyyy," he said. "You must be Mike Longridge."

He stuck out his hand. "I'm Rick, and this is my wife Maggie. We run this program. Welcome to Explore Orientation Day."

Maggie shook my hand too. She had a strong grip. "Here are a few things to get you started." She plopped a stack of handouts and a fruit bar in my hands. "Just make yourself comfortable. We're so glad you're here." Maybe *they* were glad I was here, but I wasn't. I looked up from below my pulled-up hood. At the front of the room, a big whiteboard said, *Welcome to Explore*. Below that, in even bigger writing: *DISCOVER YOUR POTENTIAL*.

A girl next to me nudged me in the ribs with a bony elbow. Hard. "Would you like crackers with that cheese?" she said, pointing at the whiteboard and rolling her eyes.

She was cute, with long black hair and perfect skin. She was the kind of girl who would never give me the time of day. Was she really talking to me? I glanced around the room to see if anyone else noticed. I could feel my cheeks burning.

"Whatever," I grunted, then slumped in my seat.

"Whatever *you*, Hooded Fang," she said, smiling. "Just trying to make conversation." She shrugged and turned back to her friends.

I flipped through my handouts. Groups of happy-looking students kayaked, rock climbed and skied across the cover of the pamphlet. *Explore changed my life,* it said underneath a photo of three wholesome groupies. *I met lots of new friends and had so many unbelievable experiences.*

Everyone else in the room was chatting in little groups. They all came from different high schools in the Okanagan because they're outdoorsy keeners. They were here because they love hiking and classifying plant species and whatever else Granolas like to do.

But why was I here? Because Lardface and her cronies didn't know what else to do with me.

I had my first meeting with Officer "Lardface" Lando within days of moving to the new town. *Officer Lando,* it said on her office door, *High School Community Liaison.* That's when she told me about the "amazing" Explore program. She gave me a whole spiel about perfect attendance, participation in all group activities and a good attitude.

"Three strikes and you're out though, buddy," she had said through a mouthful of expensive dental work. "Otherwise it's off to the Derbin day program with you."

The Explore program was five months of outdoor activity followed by five months of regular school classes. I knew about Derbin already, 'cause Cam went there a couple of years ago. They have to pick up garbage at playgrounds and stuff like that. It sounded horrible. But being forced to climb mountains with a bunch of hippies didn't sound so great either. Officer Lardface got me set up with English and math tutors, reminding me all the while that I was a good kid who falls in with the wrong peer groups.

I'd heard that one before. It was easy to find guys to hang out with. Whenever Dad and I moved to a new town, I just rode my BMX to the corner store and saw who was there. Before this summer I never did anything super bad, just keyed some cars and tagged some buildings downtown. We got caught sometimes, but the cops usually thought I was following along, and nothing happened to me. *You have an innocent face,* someone told me once. That didn't work last time though.

So I had no choice. I was stuck with this Explore program whether I liked it or not. Okay, so five months of not having to sit in math class sounded pretty sweet. But once again, my fate was decided by a clueless grown-up with a coffee mug on her desk that said *Fill your day with sunshine.*

My dad didn't care either way. "Just don't come running to me every time you need money to fix your canoe paddle," he'd said, cracking open a beer and turning back to his hockey game.

"Okay, folks, let's get started." Rick and Maggie bounded up to the whiteboard. "Let's go around the room and introduce ourselves. Tell everyone what school you're from and what brings you to Explore. Lisa, why don't you start?"

"I'm Lisa Park," the cute girl beside me said. "I'm from Westview Secondary. I *love* skiing and I can't wait to go up to the Blanket Glacier. Woohoo!"

Was she ever perky. A ripple of excitement and some other "woohoos" went through the room.

I was next. My heart started beating like crazy. I hate talking in class. I always say something dumb. Maybe if I looked down they'd just skip over me.

"Mike?" Maggie said. They weren't going to let me get away with it.

"Uh, I'm Mike Longridge. I'm not from any school. I just moved here in the summer. I'm not sure why I'm here, I guess." The Granolas looked at me and half smiled. Tough crowd. I looked down and started to doodle on my jeans with my pen.

I tuned out the rest of the introductions. After that, Rick and Maggie talked about the program and the plan for the rest of the week. When I could, I glanced over at Lisa.

"Okay, gang," Maggie said after a while. "It's snack time. Let's take fifteen minutes."

Snack time? Seriously? What was this— kindergarten? I glanced around. Everyone was digging into their Mountain Equipment Co-op backpacks. Bananas, homemade sandwiches and salads were pulled out. All I had was a half-empty bottle of flat Coke from the back of the fridge and a bag of chips. Oh yeah, and the fruit bar. I ripped open the bag of chips.

"Wow," a familiar voice beside me said, "you have the longest eyelashes I've ever seen." Out of the corner of my eye, I could see that Lisa's face was about two inches from mine.

"Whoa!" I jumped and leaned back in my chair. Those Granolas had no boundaries. But then again, I'd never had a girl as gorgeous as her that close to me before. Let alone complimenting me on my freakin' eyelashes.

"Want some of my sandwich, Longridge? I see you don't have much going on in the food department."

"Uh, no thanks."

"You don't talk much, do ya? That's cool. You're the strong silent type. Want to sit with us?"

She and her friends shuffled their chairs to make room for me. I had no idea why this Granola girl was trying to be friends with me. *Watch out for those hippie types*, Dad had said last night. *All that "love and rainbows" crap. Your little outdoor program will be crawling with 'em.*

"No, I'm okay." I pulled my hood up again.

Just as Maggie and Rick stood up to do some more talking, a guy wearing an Adidas jacket and jeans shuffled in.

"Ah, you must be Chris," Rick said, ignoring the new kid's lateness. "Great to have you here. Make yourself comfortable." He plopped the requisite stack of handouts and fruit bar into Chris's hands.

Chris grunted something and dropped the fruit bar back on Rick's desk. He slumped down a couple of desks away from me.

I smiled inside my hoodie. Maybe Chris and I had a few things in common.

chapter two

It's been the same my whole life, seems like. Whenever I see the stacks of unpaid bills start to pile up, I know that pretty soon Dad's going to say it's time to pack up and leave. He always calls it a "fresh start."

"Time to try our old tricks on some new dogs, Mikey."

I've heard it all a million times.

Then we run to the next place, and somehow Dad opens up another one of his pubs. It's always the same: waitresses with cut-off jean shorts who call me "honey" and Dad joking with all the drunks at the bar. Me and Dad living in some dump of a motel nearby.

Pub life was fun when I was a kid. I ate deep-fried everything and ice cream whenever I wanted. I beat guys four times my age at pool. Dad and I had a whole system worked out in case the cops showed up. A twelve-year-old kid wiping tables and selling smokes in a pub isn't cool with everyone, especially law-enforcement types. Anytime someone suspicious came in, one of Dad's regulars would make a hand signal. Then I'd hide in the closet or run out the back door. I used to find those moments pretty exciting. But they aren't so fun anymore.

Sometimes Dad has one of his waitresses over for a "visit." When he does, it's pretty obvious that I'm not welcome.

"Hey, Mikey, Katie and I need some alone time."

"Hey, Mikey, Roxy and I are having a special visit. Just the two of us."

This is usually followed by Katie or Roxy giggling like crazy. During those times, I usually go running. I just run, run, run until I can't run anymore. I don't have special running shoes or clothes or anything. I just head out the door in whatever I'm wearing, even if it's pajama pants and bare feet. I don't feel anything while I'm running. My legs just take over, and I can sail. Once, when we lived in Maple Ridge, I ran all the way from our motel to the town dump. The next week when my dad and I drove there to try and scrounge up some furniture, I realized that I'd run fifteen miles there and back.

Our last big move had been really bad. Dad got beat up, and we left that night with just a few things we could load into his truck. Dad didn't even have time for the "fresh start" speech, just a gruff "We're going. Now."

And here we are in Oliver. Dad works at a pub. He doesn't own it. A good idea. I don't have to wash dishes and bus tables anymore. The whole thing is okay with me, considering that I messed up pretty bad in the last town.

I don't really remember when I started "participating in illegal activities," as Lardface would say. It seems like one day I was playing with my toy trucks, and then the next thing I knew, I was in Stan's Market, stuffing comic books and dirty magazines under my shirt. The older kids at Jackson Park paid big cash for those. That was my big break into the world of thievery. But it's not like I got a rush out of doing it, like some of the other guys did. I just didn't have anything else to do.

The whole thing had been Cam's idea. He said he needed money. We were sitting on the curb outside the 7-Eleven with Ty and Derek, drinking Slurpees.

Before I knew it, we were standing at the back of a house around the corner.

"Mike, you're good at climbing stuff," said Cam. "You go first. Jam the window open."

Everyone always did whatever Cam said. I looked up. The window wasn't that far.

Using the drainpipe and the wood siding for grips, I scaled the side of the house and jammed the window open with my pocket knife. I can't say my dad never gave me anything useful.

As soon as I let the other guys in, everyone scattered to different rooms. Derek shouted when he found a box of jewelry. *Probably rhinestones,* I thought. Ty and Cam unplugged the TV and the stereo. Derek loaded up with CDs and more jewelry.

I just stood there in the kitchen. School photos of little kids framed the kitchen sink. A sign that said *Fran's Kitchen* hung above the stove. I figured we were in someone's grandma's house.

I've never seen four guys move faster than when we heard the car in the driveway. Ty threw open the kitchen window, taking the stereo with him. As I jumped out I accidentally knocked over a pot of yellow flowers. It smashed onto the clean white floor. I'm still not sure why I did it, but I climbed back inside to clean up the mess.

I heard "What is he doing?" coming from outside as I frantically wiped up the dirt. My buddies took off. I got caught, dishcloth in hand. I never ratted the other guys out. It's just not an honorable thing to do.

The authorities—aka Officer Lardface—found me almost as soon as Dad and I moved to Oliver. She got my file from my old liaison officer when Dad registered me for school. That was how I started having the weekly meetings with Officer Lardface, and that was how I ended up at Explore.

chapter three

"Okay, folks, we're going to jump right in with a game of Predator and Prey," Maggie said. She was standing on some tree roots so that she could see everyone. For such a tiny lady, she sure looked tough.

It was our first day at the wilderness site, our home base for the next five months. Other than a phone call at the crack of dawn, Lardface didn't have to come to my house that day. I even brushed my teeth before I ran the five miles to the site. But not because I was excited to start identifying bear crap or anything. It was because of Lisa.

I scanned the crowd, looking for her. She and another girl were sharing a juice box near the front of the group.

"This team-building exercise will warm you up and help you get to know each other better," Rick said.

I groaned. Team building? These teacher types were always into everyone getting to know each other. The Granolas were gazing up at Rick and Maggie, their faces shining. Except Chris, who looked like he'd had a rough night. I jogged over to stand near him at the back of the group.

"Why're you here?" I whispered.

"This or Derbin," he grunted, not looking at me.

"Same here," I said. "Wonder if anyone else here has that problem."

Chris surveyed the group. "Doubtful."

The corners of our mouths went up. Chris started to laugh, but ended up having a coughing fit instead.

"Here's how it works," Maggie was saying from her perch. "Some of you are predator animals, like eagles, wolves and bears. Some of you are prey animals, like chipmunks and deer."

Chris snickered. "Chipmunks."

Rick held up a green armband with a drawing of a rabbit on it. "You'll get these armbands. Not all of you are predator or prey animals. Two of you will be diseases, which can harm anyone. When you see a disease, run like heck."

Maggie walked around, handing out maps and armbands. "The object of the game for the prey is to visit all ten feeding stations and collect food tickets from each one. Prey, you are holding maps of the entire site. These show elevations and landmarks so that you can find the feeding stations."

I glanced down at my map in panic. All those lines and circles—I had no clue how to read the thing. The Granolas were all looking at their maps and pointing around the site as if they knew exactly what was going on. Some of them even pulled out compasses. They were all experts already.

"And predators and diseases," Rick said, "your goal is to tag your prey and collect their life tickets. Each prey animal gets life tickets that clip on your belt. You can't tag the same prey twice."

I hated games. They made me nervous. I always worried I'd get the rules wrong and then get laughed at.

I glanced over to see what armband Lisa got.

A deer. Same as me.

Chris got a chipmunk.

"Remember, it's a good idea to team up with other predators or other prey," Rick said. "There's strength in numbers. Except if you're a chipmunk. Teaming up with another chipmunk won't do a dang bit of good."

Maggie held up an air horn. "When I sound the horn, the prey get a running start. When I sound the horn again, it's the predators' turn. The third time, the diseases are on the loose."

A girl with blond dreadlocks giggled with her friend. They both had disease armbands on.

"I can run away from you any day, gangrene!" It was Lisa. Beautiful *and* funny.

"You have two hours to play," Maggie continued. "Have fun."

Hoooooonnnk. First air horn. I waited to see what Chris would do, but he just stood there, slouched against a tree.

The Granola prey tore off in every direction, maps in hand. Lots of them already seemed to be in pairs. I saw Rick start to stride over to Chris and me. We were still rooted to the spot.

But then I did what I usually did in these situations. I began to run. I just spun around and ran into the trees, trying to make sense of my map as I dodged branches.

Hoooooonnnk. Second air horn. Predators. I could hear more crashing through the bushes as the wolves and bears and cougars made their way toward us. I never thought I'd be so scared of a bunch of hippies.

I ducked behind a big stump, totally breathless.

I looked up. A feeding station was right ahead of me. I could run there in twenty seconds.

The leaves crunched beneath my feet as I slowly stood up.

"Hi-ya!" I felt a swift tap on my left shoulder.

It was the dreadlocked disease. How did she get there? If I had been running she never would have caught me.

"I'll take one of those precious life tickets," she said, holding out a small hand. "Bwa ha ha, now you only have one." She clipped it to her belt and ran off.

This is why I hated games. I've never been any good at them. I have no strategy.

"Feeding station, feeding station," I chanted to myself.

No one but me had found feeding station nine yet. I grabbed one of the food tickets and stared at my map again, hands shaking. Predators weren't allowed to hover around the feeding stations, so I had a minute.

I could feel the adrenaline racing through me. I couldn't believe I lost a life ticket in the first two minutes of the game.

Wait a minute. Was I actually buying into this? I heard more crashing through the bushes and a girl's laughter. "Can't catch me, I'm the Gingerbread Man!"

It was Lisa. At feeding station nine.

"Yo! Hooded Fang!" She grabbed my hip and spun me around. Oh my god, she touched me. "Lost a life already, I see."

She already had two feeding-station tickets and both her life tickets dangling from her belt.

"Uh...how come you—you're not paired up with anyone?" I said.

"He speaks!" She grinned. "I like to be a free agent. But I also like to help out my own species. And you, my friend, need help. Quick!"

Predators were on their way. Lisa grabbed my arm. Her hair flicked in my face as we ran. I didn't mind.

"I know a place we can hide," she said.

She pulled me around the corner to a hollow with moss hanging all around it.

We knelt and she pulled out her map. "Okay, fellow deer, we've got to backtrack to the last two stations. You've got to get caught up. See, here's number seven. I was just there. It's over the little bridge. See? Here."

She pointed at the map. Why can't maps have *you are here* magically written on them?

Lisa looked at me with those big brown eyes. "So which direction is that?"

Was she testing me? "Well, I don't, uh..." *Run. Just run.*

"That's okay. My dad taught me everything I know about maps. It takes time to learn." She pulled her compass out of a small black bag around her waist. "Right now we're facing north, and the bridge is west."

Lisa showed me the compass and the map. I still didn't get it, but it was nice of her to show me.

"Let's go!"

On the way to feeding station seven, we were caught between a wolf and a bear. Lisa darted into the bushes, shouting, "Mike, turn right, you're almost there!"

The boy bear was only a few steps away. So was the wolf.

"I've got you now, deer!" The bear shouted. He whipped out his arm. Too close.

Run. Just run.

I leaped over a fallen log, which blocked the predators for a second.

Feeding station seven. I made it. I grabbed the food ticket. Now I had two!

Then I got to stations six, four and three.

"Wow, can you ever run, Longridge!" Lisa said on the way to feeding station two.

And then...oh *crap*. Three cougars, right in our path.

"We'll go around," I breathed to Lisa, making a swift left turn.

I ran like heck. I found myself laughing my head off all the way. Those cougars were in the dust. I couldn't remember the last time I laughed like that.

Lisa turned and winked as she grabbed us each a food ticket.

I liked this game.

chapter four

I was impressed that I ended Predator and Prey with one life ticket and all my food tickets except one. Thanks to Lisa.

After the game ended, I slunk off on my own again. Lisa sat in a big circle with her friends, laughing and talking.

Chris didn't play, in any sense of the word.

"Yeah, I messed up my leg last week," he said.

"That sucks."

"Not really. At least I didn't have to run around in the woods and scavenge for roots and berries." He looked at me like I was a traitor to guys like us.

"Whatever. It was okay," I said.

Chris snorted.

Rick and Maggie were handing out orange jackets. They were Gore-Tex, with the Explore logo embroidered on them.

"Here you go, Mike," Rick said. "Medium, right?"

I'd never worn a single scrap of Gore-Tex before. It felt weird to put the jacket on, but also good somehow.

Chris scrunched his up and sat on it. He glanced at me and raised an eyebrow.

My fingers flew to the zipper on my jacket. What was up with me? First the game, now the jacket.

The other kids were putting their jackets on too, smiling their wholesome smiles.

Maggie wrangled us all together. "Group photo, Explorers!"

Lisa pulled on my sleeve. "Look at *you*! You look so cute in water-resistant, man-made fabric." She tugged me into the middle of the group.

Maggie got us all to say "Explore Sixteen rules!" The voices chimed all around me.

"Check the Explore Sixteen Facebook page later today," said Rick. "It'll be up. First of many, I'm sure."

Facebook? I didn't even have e-mail. I wasn't very good with that sort of thing.

After the photo, Rick and Maggie gave us a tour of the site. It was pretty nice, like a fancy campsite.

"All of these additions, like the carved benches, the trails, the firepits," Maggie said, "were made by other Explore classes."

"You'll leave a lasting impression too," said Rick.

Chris stretched and let out a massive yawn.

"Are we keeping you up, Chris?" Maggie said.

He leaned back, arms crossed. "When does this get fun? So far this whole crock is nothing to get excited about."

Twenty Granola faces spun around and stared at Chris. It's just not worth it to lip off in Explore. I had a feeling Chris didn't care.

Rick did the wise thing and ignored him. "Well, everyone," he said, rubbing his hands together. "Now's the moment you've all been waiting for. In the right-hand pocket of your jackets, you'll find the schedule of activities for this semester."

A buzz went through the crowd as everyone ripped into their pockets.

I waited a minute before I slowly reached in.

Rick and Maggie spent some time going over the stuff we'd need for all the outdoor trips. There was hiking, rock climbing, kayaking and backcountry skiing. Did these people ever *stop*?

Rick had already told me and Chris that there was a cupboard full of equipment we could borrow. He said it nicely, but he still meant that it was a cupboard for the poor kids.

A pinecone hit me on the leg. I looked up. It was Chris.

"Me and some of my buddies are gonna hang out tonight," he said. "Wanna come?"

"Uh, sure."

"Kay. Meet us at the Sev at, like, eight."

He walked away, leaving his Explore jacket all scrunched up where he had been sitting on it.

The other kids were standing up too. It was the end of the day.

"Hey." It was Dreadlocked Disease– Kayla, I think her name was.

I couldn't think of anything to say. I guess "Hey" back would have worked.

"Sorry for taking your life tag earlier. But it's all part of the game, right?" she said.

"Yeah."

"Some of us are going to the Green Room later for coffee. Lisa's going to sing at the open mic. Want to come?"

Why, oh why, are they trying to be friends with me? I've never had to fend off so many hippies and keeners. Or any at all, actually.

"No, I'm already busy," I said. "But, uh, thanks." Darn, I was going to miss Lisa singing.

"Oh, okay, that's cool. Some other time." Kayla turned and skipped back to the circle.

I ran all the way home. I kept my new jacket on the whole time.

"Jeezus, have they already got you in their cult uniform?" I had just slammed in through the back door. My dad cracked open a Budweiser and leaned back in his old brown easy chair. How many towns had we lived in, and that thing followed us everywhere.

I headed for the fridge. I squirted ketchup on two hot dog buns and plopped them on a paper towel. Dinner.

Dad had the football game on. As usual, we didn't have much to say to each other.

After a few beers Dad started to loosen up. "So, what do they make you do in Hippieville? Have a love-in and sing 'Kumbaya'?"

"Nah," I grunted.

"I give it a week. Then you give up. That's how it's always been with you, Mikey."

I didn't say anything. Just chewed on my hot dog bun and thought about Lisa. I imagined her with her eyes closed, strumming a guitar. That was nice. I leaned back and thought about that for a bit.

I woke up at twenty to eight. All of a sudden I didn't really feel like going to meet up with Chris. My Dad was snoring in his chair, his head slumped to the side.

I looked around the apartment. McDonald's take-out bags covered the table. Unread newspapers and pizza boxes were all over the floor.

I had to get out of there. I might as well head for the Sev.

Chris and his buddies, Chad and Jer, pulled up in front of the 7-Eleven after I'd been waiting a while. The introductions didn't take long.

We headed down 362nd Avenue past the pub and the Laundromat and the Green Room. I craned my neck and saw the Explorers in there. The place was all done up with twinkling lights. They looked pretty cozy.

I felt a punch on my shoulder. "Oh, would Mikey rather hang out with the patchouli-wearing wonders?"

Chad and Jer started laughing.

"Although a couple of those girls are pretty hot," Chris said. "Like that Chinese chick. Totally smokin'."

He was talking about Lisa. *My* Lisa. I felt a hotness from the back of my neck to my scalp.

"She's Korean." Actually, Lisa was part Korean. I remembered her saying that her mom was from Holland.

"Since when do you care?" Chris frowned.

"Where are we headed?" I asked. "The pits?"

"Nope," Chris said, looking toward the Green Room. "Somewhere better."

I got a sick feeling in my gut all of a sudden.

Run. Just run.

"Uh, I gotta go."

"Suit yourself," said Chris.

When I got home, the game was still on. It was in overtime.

"That was quick," Dad said, jolting awake as I sat down, breathing hard.

"Yeah."

I was the last to arrive at the Explore site the next morning. The place was trashed. The carved wooden bench was tipped over and bashed in on one side. Two other benches were covered with spray paint. Cans and other crap were everywhere. The other Explorers were already putting the garbage into plastic bags.

They all looked at me like I had just killed someone's kitten. Worst of all, Officer Lardface was there with Rick and Maggie. They had "concerned adult" looks on their faces.

"Mike, can we chat with you for a minute?"

They thought I had something to do with it. Rick said that Chris and his buddies had been caught after a farmer in the area called the cops. Apparently someone had seen me with Chris last night.

"No!" I said. Too loudly. "I mean, I was only with him for, like, half an hour. I made it home to watch overtime with my dad!"

Rick, Maggie and Lardface exchanged glances. They didn't look convinced. And why would they be? I was headed straight for Derbin, like Chris. There would be no Lisa at Derbin. The sick feeling in my gut came back.

Officer Lardface decided to take me back to her office "for a chat."

It took a while, but I finally convinced her that I didn't do it. I think in a moment of weakness I might have even said something about liking Explore so far. She phoned my dad, who probably grunted something about me having been home the night before.

I got back to the site in perfect time for the afternoon cross-country run. About two minutes into the run, I felt a flick on my shoulder. It was Lisa, of course. She ran easily beside me.

"Hey, Hooded Fang. I knew you didn't do it. I was never worried, even for a minute. I'm glad you're staying. You spice things up around here. If it wasn't for you, we'd just be a bunch of hemp-wearing bohos with no perspective."

I managed a small grin. We ran together for a while, over the hill and around the bend near the river.

chapter five

"On belay!"

"Climb when ready!"

The Granola voices rang out around me.

I had a harness and rubber shoes on. I had tied my figure-eight knot onto the ring on the crotch area of my harness. Great. I was wearing a big white helmet and a contraption that looked like a diaper.

We'd spent the last two days learning all about rock climbing. My head was full of information about ropes, knots and carabiners—metal hooks that hold the safety ropes. There was the three-point hold—two feet and one hand or two hands and one foot on a secure hold at the same time—and belaying. You have a belay partner who controls your safety rope, which is anchored to the top of the rock. The belay partner stands at the bottom to "offer encouragement and ensure climber safety." That's how Maggie put it.

What the heck sort of word was *belaying*, anyway? Sounded a little dirty to me. "Rock climbing is like chess and gymnastics put together," Maggie told us. "It takes mental *and* physical power to be a good climber."

"And climbing is all about teamwork," Rick chimed in. "You'll need to have good communication with your belayer."

Dreadlocked Disease, Kayla, was my partner. Perfect. I couldn't look like an idiot in front of a cute girl.

Kayla already had the belay rope firmly in her hands, ready to go.

Lisa was a few feet away, already making her way up the rock like a spider.

"Remember, you have to step up before you can reach up," our cheerleader Maggie was saying. "Find a good foothold."

All around me Explorers were finding footholds and cracks for their fingers to fit in. Had everyone except me done this before?

"Okay, let's go!" For a kittens-and-rainbows type, Dreadlocks sure was impatient. "I see a good hold for your right hand. Jutting out there."

I tore my eyes away from Lisa. My heart was beating fast. I reached up slowly. *Ow.* It felt like my fingers were being scraped off as I tried to lift myself up.

I grunted. I groaned. Quietly, to myself. Now I had scraped up my other hand on the sharp rock. The sun was beating down on my back. I felt a trickle of sweat make its way down my nose.

Why was I doing this? Picking up garbage at Derbin would be better than this. I could sit around, joke with my buddies, watch TV. Chris was probably doing that right about now.

I didn't know why I bothered trying. If I didn't try, I wouldn't fail.

"Mike, you're doing it!" Kayla shouted.

Was I? All of a sudden, I lost hold. My left foot slipped, then my right.

My stomach jolted as I fell. I whacked my leg and cut my left hand. My fingers grabbed at the rock, but I couldn't find a place to hang on. I panicked. I was going to be crushed at the bottom of—

"Mike! Mike!" *Snap.* I dangled in the air by my straps. It was Dreadlocks. "Open your eyes! You only fell about two feet!"

I opened one eye and looked around. Oh. Right.

"You okay, Mike?" Rick asked.

"Yeah, I think I—"

My feet scrabbled at the rock. I had nowhere to go. It was useless.

I couldn't do this. In my head I could hear my dad's words. *I give it a week. Then you give up. That's how it's always been with you, Mikey.*

Well, maybe I *was* giving up. I took off my helmet and threw it down.

Kayla sighed and let the rope go slack.

"Mike, I'm sorry," she said as I hopped to the ground. "We could try again."

I brushed past Dreadlocks and plopped down on a stump. If only I had a hood.

"Okay, good job, everyone! Let's switch partners." Maggie clapped her hands. "Five minutes, guys."

Lisa skipped over to my stump.

"I'd like to go with Longridge here, if that's okay." She sat down next to me and rested her elbow on my shoulder.

"Lisa, I don't think I—"

She smiled. Such perfect teeth. "No worries, Road Runner. It's scary the first time. How are your scrapes?"

Road Runner. I kinda liked it. "Okay, I guess."

"First couple times, I lost my holds completely too."

"When was that, when you were three?"

"Now, don't get all grumpy," Lisa said with a fake pout. "You can do it, Mike. I know you can."

There was something about how she said it. She really thought I *could* do it. Could I?

Then you give up. That's how it's always been with you.

But this was only the beginning. We still had kayaking, backcountry skiing and outdoor survival. There were so many more things to learn, so many more things I would suck at.

"Tell you what," said Lisa, "I feel like climbing some more. How about if you belay for me?"

"No. I'm done. I'm outta here."

"Whatever, Longridge. You are not! I'll be over there getting your rope ready."

"No, really. I'm leaving," I said. But she wasn't taking me seriously.

I didn't move. Yup, I had decided. It was Derbin for me.

The sight of Lisa uncoiling that rope though, ponytail swinging...

Next thing I knew I was holding the belay rope for her. *I'll just help her out for a few minutes,* I thought. *And then I'll go.*

Lisa seemed to find holds no problem. She made everything look so easy.

I let out the rope for her as she went up.

"Make sure your climber is safe," Rick had said yesterday. "Watch him or her at all times." I sure didn't mind watching Lisa at all times.

"Thanks, Mike!" Lisa called out. "Way to belay!"

I leaned back, the rope firm and taut in my hands. I felt like Lisa's protector. This was a pretty good gig.

Not that Lisa needed a protector. Her long legs stretched up easily as she climbed to the next ledge. Was she ever flexible.

Before I knew it though, it was my turn again. Lisa had just rappelled down the twenty-foot rock face and wasn't fazed at all.

"Your turn, Road Runner. Tie your knot."

Run away. Just go.

"Just think of it as climbing a tree," Lisa said, looking hopeful. "You climbed trees when you were a kid, didn't you?"

I stared up at the Godzilla rock and took a deep breath.

I thought of all the trees I had ever climbed.

And then I got a flash of wide cedar siding and an old gray drainpipe. Right foot on the pipe bolt, left hand on the siding ridge. This was just like the time I climbed in the window of that house in Vernon.

My right hand found a small crack in the rock. I jammed my fingers in and went a little higher. Foot, foot, hand. Hand, hand, foot.

"Yay, Mike!"

Lisa sounded so happy.

I was ready to get this party started.

chapter six

"So, she's hot?" asked Cam.

"Totally," I said.

"If she's so hot, why would she like *you*, dude?"

"What's that supposed to mean?"

Cam let out a huge watery burp. Right into the phone. He'd always been a classy guy. "Sounds like she's totally out of your league—Get him! Aw, crap!"

Cam's Xbox was blipping and bleeping in the background. I could hear the click of the controller. He was probably sucking at *Grand Theft Auto*, as usual.

"Yeah, but—"

"I so had him! Mike, you should have seen the move I just made. Man! Oh, come *on*...Hey, guy, I gotta go."

It was another of our two-minute conversations.

Why would she like you, *dude*? Why was I friends with Cam anyway? He was probably sitting in his basement, his gut hanging out, playing video games all day.

I went to my room and flopped on my bed with a groan. Cam was such a jerk. He didn't know that Lisa laughed at my jokes and looked me in the eye. She actually seemed to like being around me. Knowing that I'd see Lisa at Explore every day kind of kept me going.

But maybe she was too hot for a loser like me. *She likes you. No, she doesn't. She likes you. No, she doesn't.* I should have been pulling petals off a daisy or something.

No, this was the new Mike. The new

Mike had the guts to ask out the girl of his dreams.

It took a couple days. There were always so many people around. I came close to getting her alone a few times, but someone else would always barge in. Finally I had my chance. Friday before our morning run, I saw Lisa sitting on the grass, lacing up her sneakers. Alone.

Okay, Mike, go for it. She likes you. For some unknown reason, she likes you. I felt sweat drip down my back and into my shorts. Ugh.

I tried to act casual. "Hey, Lisa."

"Yo, Longridge! What's shakin'?"

"Well, uh, I was wondering if you, if you..." *What an idiot.* I hadn't even thought of where I wanted to ask her to go. I knew I'd say something dumb.

Lisa smiled. "What's up?"

"Uh, I was wondering if you wanted to go to the Green Room for coffee after school."

She pulled her lace tight with a swift tug. "Today? Oh, I have volleyball."

Volleyball? She spends all week in Explore, hiking up mountains and learning outdoor survival skills, and she still goes to volleyball on Friday nights?

"Uh, maybe tomorrow?"

"We've got the big game this weekend. You should come!"

This girl *was* a crazy, type-A Wonder Woman. Most weekends I slept until two in the afternoon and then watched TV all day.

"Yeah, um, okay. Well, how about Monday? For coffee."

"Monday?" She looked up for a minute. "Monday...cool! I'll invite Kayla and Jen." She turned to the rest of the group over by the tree stump and started to call them over. "Hey, Kayla—"

This was not going as I had planned. "No! Lisa!" She looked up at me, a little stunned. I sat down on the grass next to her. I was *doing* this. "Actually, I was hoping that maybe it could just be you and me."

"Just you and me," she repeated. Lisa's forehead wrinkled up for a second. That was so cute. "Oh. *Oh.*"

Lisa looked away, fiddling with the laces on her sneakers. Then she stood up quickly. So did I. "Um...actually, I might have something on Monday night. I'll have to check my schedule and let you know. I just get so booked up. Sorry, Mike."

Mike. She never called me Mike.

Oh crap, what did I say wrong? Or maybe she did have to check her schedule.

Lisa took off, racing to catch up with Kayla.

"So Mr. Longridge. Here we are again." There were those teeth again too. Unfortunately, right after the run I had my meeting with Lardface. At least she always had candy on her desk. Jolly Ranchers, my favorite. "How was the white-water trip last week?"

"Pretty good."

"Maggie mentioned that you flipped your kayak. Did you get the hang of it after that?"

"Uh, I guess."

"And Rick said that you're really coming along in orienteering. Can be tricky to read those compasses, can't it?"

What, do Rick and Maggie call Lardface every night and give her a blow-by-blow account of Mike Longridge's Day at Explore? *And then he had lunch...it was a stale peanut butter sandwich. And then Mike went to the bathroom. He crumples rather than folds his toilet paper. And then he...*

I wouldn't be surprised.

"I hear you've been hanging out with Tim. He's a good guy. Helps out at the pancake breakfast every year."

I nodded. Jeez, these people *do* know everything about everyone. I bet she also knew that I slept with a teddy bear named Tiggy when I was three.

"Maggie also said that you spend a lot of time with a certain"–Lardface looked down at her notepad–"Lisa Park. How's *that* going, Mike?"

I didn't say anything. There were some things authority figures didn't need to know. Also, I was feeling kind of tortured about the whole Lisa-checking-her-schedule thing.

When I got back to the Explore site, it was our third day of archery practice. I'd come close to a bull's-eye a couple of times.

Lisa was standing with Kayla and Jen. They didn't see me. I ducked behind a tree and pretended to tie my boot.

"Seriously?" Jen's squeaky voice.

"So what did you say?" Kayla. Her voice wasn't quite so squeaky.

"I just told him I had to check my schedule."

"Hmmm."

"Well, I had to think fast after I realized he wanted it to be just me and him."

"What was he thinking?" Kayla said. "I mean, you're so totally out of his league. You could have any guy in the whole school."

"Well, I mean, I like him as a friend." Lisa buried her face in her hands. "Oh my god, you guys, I'm such an idiot! I led him on, completely."

Jen put her arm around Lisa's shoulders. "Lis, sometimes you're just way too nice."

"I know. My mom says I like to help out the injured birds."

"Yeah," Jen said, "but you don't realize that when a girl like you talks to a boy like *him*, of course he's going to like you as more than a friend."

"Why don't you just tell him you have a boyfriend?"

"Kay, I don't want to lie."

"Well, that's the easiest way out of it," said Kayla.

"No, I'll think of something else."

They walked away, down the path. Their voices got lost in the trees.

God. I was such an idiot. She didn't like me at all. I was just her latest charity case—an injured bird, a complete and utter loser.

A boy like him. *Out of his league.* Those girls were worse than Cam.

My heel dug into the soggy ground. I kicked up a huge hunk of grass, then another. Sometimes destruction could be so satisfying. Worms dangled out the bottom of the dirt chunks. *I bet worms don't have to worry about rejection.*

"Hey, Mike, you coming? We're heading over to the field." Tim and Rick walked by with bags full of arrows slung over their shoulders.

I never wanted to show my face to Lisa or Kayla or Tim or anyone in Explore ever again. But I blindly put one foot in front of the other and made it over to the archery field. I hauled a bunch of arrows out of the bag and grabbed a bow, slamming it into my knee as I yanked at it.

"Mike, you okay?" Tim asked. "You seem a little out of it."

"Yup."

Shoot. Try again. Shoot. Try again. Every time, my arrows sailed past the target. They didn't even come close.

So Lisa didn't like me after all. *Just as a friend.* That's the worst phrase ever invented.

I squinted at the target. *Pretend the target is every guy that can have Lisa, the quarterback and the track star and all those taller, smarter, cooler guys than me.* I hated them all.

Bull's-eye.

chapter seven

The phone was ringing—and ringing and ringing. I wasn't going to answer it. I heard some mumbling and a gruff "hello" from the living room.

I rolled over and looked at the alarm clock. It was 11:22 AM.

Dad kicked my door open and clunked the phone down near my ear without saying a word. I caught a good whiff as he left. Cigarettes, beer and a bad case of BO. Gotta love how he didn't even care I wasn't at school.

"Yeah?" I mumbled into the phone.

"Mr. Longridge. You're not at school today. Are you sick?" It was Lardface, of course. Who else would it be?

"No." Darn, why did I say that? "Uh, maybe a bit."

"Unless you're puking your guts out and have a fever of a hundred and one, get your butt down there. You know the rules."

Sometimes I wondered if Officer Lardface had been in the army.

I shoved one leg out of the blankets. No, I couldn't do it. The thought of going to Explore after the whole "injured birds" scene on Friday actually did make me want to puke.

I hadn't left my room all weekend, not even for a run. I kept thinking about Lisa leaping around on the volleyball court. Her team had probably won the game. I imagined her ponytail swinging as she did a perfect serve.

I'd thought about her all weekend. I bet she hadn't thought about me.

She didn't like me. Well, she liked me "as a friend." And I still had to look at her every day and mentally drool over her. Now I really had no chance with her. I wondered if there was some way to get her to like me. Like if I suddenly got really good at everything sporty and outdoorsy. *No, Mike, don't be an idiot.*

I groaned. I had to get up. As if I was going to let Lardface come and rip me out of bed again.

I heard screechy giggling from the living room. Big Lips, Dad's new "lady friend," was here. Her name was Angie. She had this giant mouth on a pale face and wore tons of globby red lipstick. Sometimes it was on her teeth. You looked at her and the first thing you thought was *big, huge, crazy lips*. If Dad and Big Lips were going to be doing their thing all day, I definitely had to get out of there.

I dragged myself in to Explore just before tracking class. We were learning how to identify wild animals by their paw prints and poop.

"Hey, Mike, nice to see you. Glad you could make it. I tried calling you this morning, but when you didn't answer, I had to pass it along the chain of command." Rick shrugged apologetically and gave me a playful punch on the shoulder. A few of the Granolas gathered around and gave me an are-you-feeling-okay? welcome. Couldn't a guy just be miserable in peace?

Lisa didn't talk to me all afternoon. She, Kayla and Jen walked around glued together like a single-celled organism. What were those things we learned about in science last year? Oh yeah, *paramecium*. They were a really good-looking paramecium.

I stood at the back of the group, hood up.

"You okay?" Good old Tim.

"Yeah, just not feeling so good."

"You still into going up to the hill tomorrow for a little practice?" asked Tim.

"Oh, uh, yeah." Tim had offered to show me the ropes before our big five-day backcountry ski trip. Ugh. My guts tossed and turned just thinking about it.

The next day was wilderness skills. We were going to learn how to make fires using bow drills.

"In your hands you have everything you need to generate friction, heat and then fire," Maggie said. I looked at the bow with the rope attached to it. I also had a stick and a board. I was supposed to make fire with a stupid twig and a piece of rotten wood?

Rick gave us the instructions and said, "Remember, guys, it can take a while to get the fire going. Don't give up. Just keep trying."

I found a spot away from the group. I sat with my back to everyone and tried to figure out how the heck the bow and the stick worked together. A couple of minutes later I heard footsteps crunching toward me. I was pretty sure I knew who it was.

"Hey, Mike."

I didn't look up. I was starting to get the hang of spinning the stick with the bow to get the burn going. My heart was beating like crazy and I could feel my cheeks going red.

"Mike, I want to talk to you." Lisa's voice didn't sound all fun and perky like usual. It was deeper, more serious. "Can you look at me for a sec?"

I didn't say anything.

Lisa lifted one edge of my hood. "Michael Longridge, are you in there?" She took a deep breath. *Whoa, is the great Lisa Park actually feeling nervous?* "Look, I'm sorry about Friday. I didn't know what to do when you asked me out. I didn't want to hurt your feelings. But I'm just not interested in you that way."

I kept sawing away with my bow and stick, a little faster.

"But I really want to be friends."

Part of me wanted to chuck the bow drill down and shake Lisa by her pretty little shoulders, have a big freak-out over the unfairness of it all.

"I think we have a really good friendship," Lisa said. "I don't want to mess with that."

Actually, you're too ugly and dumb for a goddess like me, but I still want to torture you by hanging out with you. That's what she really meant.

She didn't know that I'd already heard all of this.

"Mike, aren't you going to say something?"

I thought I might be getting close to getting some smoke with my bow drill. I sawed even harder. I could see the steam of my breath in the cold air.

"Yup, whatever."

"So we're friends? You're okay?"

"I guess." She still had my hoodie edge lifted up. I didn't look at her. She sighed and ran back to her paramecium.

I tried for what felt like five hours to get a fire started. No spark.

At the end of the day, Rick and Maggie gathered us all together to talk about our big backcountry ski trip the next Friday. Five days in the Cascade Mountains.

We got to go up there by helicopter. That part sounded pretty cool. Usually heli-skiing is *mucho* expensive, but Rick's brother owns a helicopter so he takes the Explore kids up the mountain every year.

All I knew about telemark skiing was that it combined two of the worst things known to man: downhill skiing *and* hiking. I had never been downhill skiing, but I already knew I wouldn't like it. Telemark skiing was way too much work, in my opinion. You have to ski down these crazy backcountry hills and then hike right back up the hill and do it all over again. Yeah, looked like two tons of fun.

Rick and Maggie showed us a video that looked like it was from 1982, with a dude in a bright pink ski suit demonstrating all the moves. Unlike regular downhill skiing, in telemark skiing you have to bend your knees one at a time as you go down the hill. I didn't get it. The Granolas had probably all been skiing and hiking since they were out of diapers—probably when they were *in* diapers. Once again, I would be left out in the cold. Literally.

"It's a good thing you've got that ski thing going on tonight," my dad said when I stopped home after school for my ski stuff. "Me and Angie have been looking forward to a little alone time." He looked at Big Lips and wiggled his eyebrows in that sick way he does.

A stack of bills caught my eye as I opened the door: bank, credit cards, phone, hydro, gas. My stomach twisted.

"Dad!" I called into the living room. "You're going to pay these, right?" Things were lousy right now, for sure, but I didn't want to run away from yet another town.

There was no answer, just the TV and Big Lips's giggle. I couldn't get out of there fast enough. Tim and his older brother were waiting outside. I told him to just pull up and honk. I didn't want Tim to see the hole I lived in. Tim, Bryce and their crappy 1989 Chevette were the best things I'd seen all day.

chapter eight

On day one of the dreaded backcountry ski trip, we sat packed onto the yellow school bus. All around me the Granolas were laughing, telling jokes, crunching trail mix. I just stared out the window, completely freaked out.

The telemarking practice session with Tim had been a disaster. I'd spent more time eating snow than skiing on it. I was a total spaz on skis.

"It's okay, Mike," Tim had said. "Telemarking takes a lot of getting used to. You can't expect to learn it all in one day. Especially if you don't already know how to downhill ski."

I bet I was the only Explorer who didn't know how to ski already. Tim was a competitive ski racer *and* a champion mountain biker. I wanted to punch him in the mouth sometimes. He was way too sporty for his own good.

I didn't know how I was going to hack the ski trip. I thought about faking sick. But making an idiot out of myself on a ski hill was better than hanging out with Dad and Big Lips.

We were close to the helicopter port. We had to stop for some road construction. I saw a row of *Derbin Juvenile Facility* jackets. A bunch of Derbin kids were picking up garbage on the other side of the ditch. They were a pretty rough-looking bunch.

One of them turned around to face the bus.

Chris. I'd almost forgotten about him.

He spotted me right away. He lifted his right arm and raised his middle finger. He held it up with a calm look on his face. I don't think anyone else noticed.

The helicopter ride was just about the coolest thing ever. I was in a group with Lisa, Kayla, Jen and Maggie. We flew straight up the face of the mountain, in between the trees. It was just like in a movie, with that choppy helicopter-blade sound and everything. That helicopter had to make six trips up and down the mountain to get all of us up there.

We landed on a helicopter pad, right next to an A-frame cabin with fancy black shutters. A "Swiss-style chalet," everyone was saying. How hoity-toity. A sign next to the cabin said: *Welcome to the Cascade Mountains Heli-Ski Area.*

We were way up, almost in the clouds. It was totally unreal.

"Woohoo, backcountry!" Lisa squealed.

I had never seen such deep snow. The branches of the trees hung low, with huge white marshmallows all over them. It was just us, a cabin, lots of huge trees and tons of snow.

We hauled all our stuff inside the cabin. It had one big room downstairs with couches and a table. Upstairs there were separate boys' and girls' bedrooms with bunk beds. The only problem: no indoor toilets—outhouses only. We were going to freeze our butts off. Kayla, Tim and I went down the path next to the cabin to check them out.

"Holy crap, you guys, look at this!" said Tim, looking down the toilet into the outhouse hole.

"*Pointy* crap, more like it," said Kayla. The inside of the toilet was not the usual sloppy outhouse muck. This outhouse crap was frozen into a perfect pyramid of poop. I'd never seen anything like it.

Of course we had to call everyone else out to look at it.

When we got back into the cabin, Maggie had a fire going. Rick cooked a big pot of pasta with artichoke hearts and goat cheese. It was fancier than I usually like, but it was really good. Maybe this trip wasn't going to blow after all.

But soon enough it was time to go out in the snow.

"Okay, gang," Maggie said once we were all suited up. "Grab your partner."

I looked around. Lisa and Tim were already clowning around. Lisa used to want to be my partner. But not anymore.

Lisa had already tried to talk to me a few times that day, but I couldn't think of anything to say. There were no more cute little nicknames. No more playful slaps on the shoulder. No more partnering up. No more magic.

I was partners with Jill. She was a Granola, all right, but I could count on her to suck as much as I did at telemarking. She blabbed away at me as we put on our skis.

"This is so cool!" she said. "People pay, like, thousands of dollars to go heli-skiing. And we get to do it for free!"

At first it seemed okay. A lot of the Granolas had never been telemark skiing, either, so even they were wobbly at first. That made me feel better. Jill giggled whenever she fell down.

I felt so good about not being the only one who didn't get it that I couldn't help but laugh.

Before long, though, the Granolas started getting the hang of it. Of course they did. Even Jill started swooshing along.

And there I was, still stuck at the all-you-can-eat snow buffet.

I looked up as the Granolas glided down the hill past me, beautiful as birds. Birds wearing expensive ski gear. I was wearing a too-small jacket and bright orange ski pants from the poor kid closet. Thanks, Rick and Maggie.

I was still laying there, trying to use my poles to get up when the Granolas all turned around to start hiking back up the hill.

That's another awesome thing about telemark skiing. When you get to the bottom of the hill, there's no fancy chairlift to get you back up to the top. Nope, you have to be hardcore and hike all the way back up the hill you just skied down. You have to attach these things called skins to the bottom of your skis, which give you friction so that you can go uphill. The skins looked like long fruit roll-ups with a furry side and a sticky side. You stick the sticky side on the bottom of your ski. And you're supposed to take off one ski at a time to put them on. I had no idea how that would be possible.

I hoped that whoever invented telemark skiing died a horrible death. And if they weren't already dead, I wanted to kill them.

I wiggled my backpack off to get out my skins, which were rolled up in the front pouch. The Granolas could all balance on one ski, take off their other ski and stick the skin on. What a bunch of show-offs.

After about a million years, Rick announced that we were going back to the cabin. The plan was to ski the long way back.

"The long way back?" I moaned to no one in particular.

My soaking wet toque dripped icy water into my jacket and down my back. My hair was plastered across my forehead. My legs and arms ached from falling down so much. I probably had frostbite. This day was never, ever, *ever* going to end.

Tim, and then Kayla, skied past me. They asked if I was okay. "Yeah, yeah, I'm fine," I muttered.

I stood there watching all the Granolas get way ahead of me until they became little dots. I couldn't move. I didn't want to. I looked around. What was the *short* way back to the cabin?

Finally I started to move, one ski in front of the other. But every time I went two steps I'd fall. After five, six or maybe a hundred and fifty-six times, I just stayed down. I imagined myself freezing to death. I imagined Lisa finding me the next day, all blue and stiff.

The sky was getting darker. Soon it would be black. I heard the crunch-crunch, swoosh-swoosh of skis approaching. I tried to sit up and recover at least a little dignity. But the deep snow had me trapped.

"Mike?"

It was Maggie. She'd been behind me the whole time. Of course, she couldn't leave me to fend for myself.

"I've been keeping a respectful distance, Mike," she said, smiling. "But now it's getting dark. Need a hand?"

What Maggie really meant is that I was officially the biggest loser in the history of skiing. She towed me all the way back to the cabin. Seriously. She tied a rope around her waist and made me hang on. Like a friggin' US army tank, this tiny little lady chugged along on her skis for a good mile, with me sliding uselessly behind her.

I had never been more humiliated. This was even worse than the time in grade three when I laughed so hard at Shane Armstrong's joke about horny elephants that I peed myself. I had to wear the plaid emergency pants that everyone knew were for when people had an "accident."

The plaid pants had been bad, but being towed back to base camp in full view of all the Granolas was worse, much worse.

It took forever for the cabin to come into view. It was pitch-black by then. Through the steamy windows I saw twenty Granola faces pressed to the glass.

"Uh, Maggie...could we stop for a sec? I can do it myself now!" I let go of the rope and plopped down in the snow.

It was too late. Everyone saw stupid loser Mike getting rescued by the teacher.

The Granolas all crowded around as soon as we opened the door, with concerned looks on their shiny faces. Except Kayla, who was laughing so hard she was crying.

"Oh my god, we were so worried!" Jill— my partner who let the teacher pick up the slack—said.

"We were about to send out a search party," said Rick, putting his arm around Maggie and winking at me. Various Granolas were tugging off my toque, drying my hair, pulling off my jacket and gloves and shoving hot chocolate in my hands.

They wanted to know what had happened. They seemed to want some big story, like I fought off a bear or something. But no, it was just me being me.

"Guys, thanks for your help, but I think Mike just needs to get himself settled," Maggie said, giving me her kind smile.

I didn't want any kind smiles. I pushed past everyone and stomped to the boys' bedroom. But my legs hurt so much that I couldn't move all that fast.

As I lay in my bunk on my old sleeping bag, I heard everyone downstairs laughing and having a good time.

Someone knocked on the door and asked if I was okay. I didn't answer.

I rolled over and finally fell asleep.

I woke up a few hours later. The cabin was dead quiet. I had to pee. I hate going to the bathroom in the middle of the night, especially when it's minus-thirty outside. Maybe I could just use an old bottle or something.

I looked out the kitchen window. The snow made the world outside so bright and sparkly. Next thing I knew, I was outside wearing someone's old boots and ski jacket, freezing in my pajama pants.

The moon was like a huge spotlight on the snowy trees. That was the only light. It was the stillest, clearest night I had ever seen. The stars were amazing. There were trillions of them up there. It was like I could see the entire Milky Way.

Despite the cold, I stood there for a long time. It was just me and the stars.

chapter nine

I had no idea how I would face the world after my telemarking disaster. So I faked a headache. I'm really good at pretending to be sick. Rick gave me two aspirins and said they'd be back around noon.

I wandered around in the cabin for a while. I picked up a book, *Guinness Book of Records 1994*—a little out of date. All those records would be broken by now. I put it down. There was no TV or video games or anything. I sat on the couch and drummed on the table for a bit. I think it would be awesome to be a drummer in a punk band. I can imagine myself all sweaty, banging away on a drum kit and then partying with all the hot groupies after. That would rule. But I have no rhythm.

I stopped drumming and looked around.

It was only nine in the morning, and I was bored, bored, bored. They'd be gone for a while yet. I paced around. I looked out the window. The sun glinted off the snow on the roof of the outhouses. I glanced at my backpack and skis, neatly stacked by the door. Maggie's work, probably. I looked outside again.

Ten minutes later I was outside with all my telemarking gear on. I'm not sure why.

I took a few sliding steps out in the snow. I bailed. I took a few more steps and bailed again. My arms were killing me from falling so many times the day before. Why bother?

I clumped back to the front steps of the cabin, popped my boots out of the bindings and looked around.

What the heck. What else was I going to do? Except maybe go back inside and snoop around for Lisa's diary.

That was tempting, but no. She'd catch me and then I'd be even more of an idiot.

Maybe I could just try skiing to that tree over there. I clicked my boots into the bindings again. I slipped and slid to the tree. I made it! *Okay, now to the next tree.* I kept going, tree to tree.

After a while, I realized that I had skied quite a way and hadn't wiped out. My legs were moving without me thinking about them. My arms worked the ski poles as though I was some sort of Granola.

I turned around to see how far back the cabin was. As soon as I did that, I tipped over and got a faceful of powder.

No sweat. It was easier to get up now. My skis made that swoosh-swoosh sound. I thought if I followed the tracks, maybe I could even catch up to everyone else.

I could hear Maggie's voice: *Eventually you just catch your rhythm, and then you can sail.*

I think I was sailing. No, I was *sure* I was sailing.

I went along like that for a while. I felt pretty good.

And then I saw something.

Why was a ski sticking out from that tree? I skied up closer to check it out. It was hard to tell what was going on under the snow and all those mangled branches.

I shoved some of the branches aside. Big blobs of powdery snow slid off the tree and onto my head.

It was a tree well. Rick and Maggie had warned us about them. How did they put it? *The low-hanging branches of the tree create a sheltered area around the base of the tree where a well of loose snow can form.* It was like a big air donut around the base of a tree. If a skier accidentally falls into one of those he's pretty much dead meat.

I knelt down and cleared some of the snow away from around the ski, which was wedged in a tree branch. That ski was attached to a leg. For some reason I grabbed the leg.

"Ahhh! Oh my god!" Someone screamed. There was so much snow. I tried to clear more away. The branches scratched my face.

Kayla was stuck upside-down in the tree well. She was covered in snow. No way could she reach up to undo her bindings. She was totally trapped. I wondered how she got in there.

Okay, Mike. Think fast. Someone's hurt.

Now I know how I react in an emergency situation: with sheer panic. I had never felt my heart pounding so fast in my chest before. I stood up and whipped my head around, desperate to spot someone. I hollered for help. I shouted and yelled.

But it was just me.

"Help!" Kayla screamed.

"Um, Kayla?" I started to lean into the well and slid a bit. Crap, I didn't want both of us trapped. I scrambled up and out.

Kayla craned her neck to look up at me. "Mike! Oh god...I've been here so long—I was calling for help..." She trailed off. Maybe she had hit her head. Maybe she was losing consciousness. This wasn't good.

I tried to remember everything Maggie and Rick told us about tree wells. I never thought I'd have to deal with something like this alone. Then I heard Rick's voice in my head.

Keep talking to the trapped skier. Ask if she can move or if she is injured.

"Don't worry, I'll help you! Stay with me, Kayla!" What was I, some character in a lame Mount Everest movie? "Uh, did you hurt yourself?"

"My arm! Help, my arm...," she moaned.

Shout for help and light a flare.

I had already shouted and didn't have a flare.

Undo the victim's bindings so that she can climb out of the tree well if possible.

That should be easy. I clenched my teeth and pressed down on the toe clip to release the binding. My hands shook. Agh, it was jammed. This was worse than trying to open a pickle jar. I clamped Kayla's leg under my armpit and tried to pry open the binding. I pulled her boot right off and smacked myself in the jaw while I was at it. I tried to stuff her boot back on, still attached to the ski. I had no idea what I was doing.

There was an avalanche shovel in my backpack. Was I supposed to use that?

Kayla had stopped struggling. *Holy cow, Mike, just yank her out of there.* I grabbed on to both legs. I huffed and puffed and hauled her out of the tree well, knocking myself over.

Kayla looked pretty rough and was shivering a lot, but she was still conscious. I put my first aid blanket on her. We could thank Maggie for our backpacks full of all that gear. But what was I supposed to do now?

"I'm freezing!" Kayla kept saying.

I tucked and re-tucked the blanket around her. I felt useless.

After five, ten or maybe twenty minutes, I heard swooshing sounds in the snow.

My head snapped up. I don't know how long we'd been out there, but it felt like my entire body had frostbite. Maggie and Lisa were skiing toward us. I'd never been so happy to see them.

"Oh my god, it's Mike and Kayla!" Lisa cried. "We've been looking for Kayla for over half an hour!"

Kayla's arm wasn't broken, but she had a bad sprain. She was going to be okay. They still decided to call the medivac helicopter to come and take her to the hospital, just to be sure. It was all very dramatic.

While she was taking care of Kayla, Maggie kept talking about how brave I was.

"You really showed your true colors today. Amazing job, Mike. You saved our girl." She gave me a lot of big hugs. I've never been much of a hugger.

Back in the cabin, Rick made everyone hot chocolate with little marshmallows.

"Oh my god, Mike. I didn't see her go down. If you hadn't been there, I...I..." Lisa couldn't finish her sentence. She was crying. Big, beautiful tears slid down her cheeks. "I can't believe I let that happen. I'm so stupid. Jen and I were too busy talking to realize that Kayla wasn't with us anymore. Maggie already gave us a huge lecture about never letting your partner out of your sight. You saved Kayla's life."

Me, saving someone's life? All I did was find Kayla. I didn't really do much of anything.

Rick stood in front of the group.

"What happened today was very serious. We need to remember to look out for our partners at all times." I looked over at Lisa and Jen. They looked like little kids who had just gotten in big trouble.

"Mike showed a remarkable degree of resourcefulness and quick-thinking today," Rick continued. "He exemplifies what the Explore program is all about."

Me? *I* was the Explore poster child now?

Rick raised his mug. "To Mike."

Everyone else raised their chipped cabin mugs.

"To Mike," the Granola voices chorused.

Rick started singing, "For He's a Jolly Good Fellow," and all the Granolas chimed in. I couldn't believe it. What was this, some sort of hippie musical?

"Thanks for choosing us over juvie, Mike!" Tim broke in. What a jokester.

I found myself smiling, even with everyone staring at me.

"I've never seen you grin like that before, Longridge!" Lisa laughed and swatted me on the shoulder. She was still teary.

Longridge was back.

chapter ten

My lungs were about to pop. I could barely see with all the sweat in my eyes. The roads were icy, but I kept running. I was somewhere on the back roads of town and didn't know where I was going. I was just running. The past twelve hours had been the worst in my life. And I've had a lot of bad hours.

Most of it was a blur. I'd gotten home the night before, totally elated after the ski trip. I walked in the house and saw boxes everywhere. My dad said, like he had a hundred times before, "Time for a fresh start, Mikey." I kicked over a bunch of boxes. My dad grunted that like it or not, we were moving. To Nelson, no less. "We'll sort out school later."

I threw a beer bottle and broke the kitchen window.

"I've finally found somewhere that I belong," I'd yelled. Then I slammed the door to my room and stayed there all night too angry to change out of my clothes or sleep.

This wasn't like all the other times we moved. For once I had a reason to stay.

But now, once again, I was out running because my life was a steaming pile of crap.

I felt like breaking something other than the kitchen window. I used to love it when my buddies and I would smash car windows. Or maybe I'd go steal something. I hadn't done that in months.

An awful acid taste crept into my mouth. I ran to the nearest shrub and chucked all over it. I wiped my mouth on my sleeve and chucked again.

Okay, maybe I didn't really want to steal anything. The owner of the shrub was glaring out her living-room window at me. I took off up a gravel road. It looked peaceful up there.

"Howdy, partner, what're you doin' in these parts?" The voice surprised me. I spun around.

On no. Not Lisa. I didn't want to talk to anyone, not even her.

Lisa did a sideways jump so that she was standing right in front of me.

"How did you know it was me?" I wiped the last bit of barf from the side of my mouth.

"I was out for a walk," she said. "Recognized the hoodie."

"Oh. Yeah."

Lisa studied my face. "What's up, Longridge? Are you okay?"

"Um, no, I'm fine." *Well actually, my dad is a jerk and I just puked all over that shrub over there.*

"You don't look fine. I live near here. Wanna come over for a minute?"

This was all so weird. All of a sudden Lisa was back in my life, calling me her little nicknames. I'd been thinking about that. Was I only in her exclusive club again because I saved her friend?

I shook my head. "No. Not right now." I started running again. Lisa ran along beside me. Darn, she had me trapped.

"Seriously, dude, what's up? Are you just not in the mood to talk?"

"Yeah. I just want to go for a run."

"Okay, Longridge. See you around." She hung back and let me run ahead.

After a couple minutes I heard footsteps on gravel.

"Please?" Lisa skidded in front of me again. "We just went to Timmy's."

Call me a cheap sell, but the thought of donuts perked me up, especially after all that running.

I sunk my teeth into a Boston cream, fresh from the Tim Hortons box, so sweet and chewy and good.

"Wasn't the big snowball fight fun?"

Lisa said through her jelly donut. "That was wicked when you and Tim snuck up on Brian."

"Yeah. That was awesome."

"It'll be different when we're in regular classes in January. But at least we'll all be together."

I looked down and picked some of the icing off my donut. A coconut chocolate one this time. "I might not be there."

"What?" Boy, could she ever shriek when she wanted to. "What are you talking about?"

"My dad wants to move."

"Now? In the middle of the school year?" Lisa stood up and slammed her hands on the table. "Well, tell him you can't! You just can't! Explore needs you! Does he know that you just saved someone's *life*?" She put her hand to her forehead and started pacing around the kitchen.

I put down the rest of my donut. Since when did Explore need me? I was only there as a pity case.

"Actually, never mind. I gotta go. Thanks for the donuts." I got up to go, pulling my hood up over my eyes.

"Don't be ridiculous. Stay, and we'll figure this out."

I was already heading for the door to put my shoes on. But where was I going to go from here? Home? No. The 7-Eleven? No. Officer Lardface's office?

"Earth to Longridge!"

I realized that I had been standing by the front door, holding my right shoe and staring off into space.

She tugged off my hood and laughed. "I'm afraid I can't unleash the Hooded Fang on the world when he's this upset."

I couldn't help but smile a little. "Well, I guess I could stay for one more donut."

We were back at the kitchen table. I took a big bite of an apple fritter. I chewed it for a good long time. Lisa asked what was up again.

It all came out. I told Lisa about my messed-up life, my messed-up father and how I'm a lying, stealing juvenile delinquent. I told her I couldn't remember the names of all the towns my dad and I had lived in and how I didn't want to move again. I even threw in the part about my mom being only seventeen when she had me and that she died in a car accident when I was four. I don't think I've ever talked so long in my life. Lisa nodded the entire time.

When I finished, Lisa was staring at me. "You're not really a troublemaker though, are you? I mean, you haven't done anything to prove it so far in Explore. Maybe you're just easily influenced."

Who was she, Officer Lardface? It would be way better to be a born troublemaker rather than a by-default troublemaker. I shrugged.

But then Lisa smiled. "So I guess us Granolas finally touched your cold, hard heart, eh, Mike?"

"It took a while," I said. "But yeah."

Then I remembered about the Granolas only liking me because I saved Kayla. I asked Lisa about that.

"No! I can't believe you thought that!" I think Lisa genuinely felt bad. She paused. "Although that was pretty amazing. You pulled her right out of that tree well. *You*, Mike Longridge!" She poked her finger into my chest as she said it.

Lisa and I talked about lots that afternoon. We talked about the future. Lisa had some pretty interesting plans for after high school. She wanted to become a doctor and volunteer in orphanages in Guatemala. I always thought I'd just work in a gas station or something after graduation. Maybe I could do something cool too.

After a while Lisa stood up. "Okay, enough talking. We have to do something about this moving-away problem. I have an idea. Be right back."

Lisa jogged downstairs to the basement.

I looked around the kitchen. I'd been too wound up earlier to notice what Lisa's house looked like. It was a regular, run-of-the-mill house, with lived-in furniture and family photos. It was tidy and there were lots of books. I wondered what Lisa's bedroom looked like. I had always imagined her living in a mansion.

Lisa returned with a pad of paper and a pen.

"Okay, Longridge. You're going to do it the old-fashioned way. You're going to write your dad a letter and tell him how you feel."

"A *letter*?" What was this, a self-help seminar?

Lisa nodded. "And you're going to add this photo. I just printed it." She handed the photo to me. It was all of us Explorers up on the mountain. I was standing beside Lisa and Tim with the biggest grin on my face.

"Lisa," I said, studying the photo, "have I become a Granola? Have I totally sold out?"

Lisa laughed. "No way, José. Tie-dye and hemp jewelry will never touch your lily-white body. Besides, sold out from what? Would all the criminal losers you used to hang out with be so disappointed in you?"

I pretended to be offended. We laughed. Then Lisa got all businesslike again.

"Okay, you gotta write that letter to your dad."

"I don't know what to say."

Lisa passed the pen to me. "I'll help. You write."

If Lisa was surprised at my kindergarten writing skills, she didn't show it. It took about three hours that afternoon, but we did it. The letter had scratched-out parts all over it, and probably had tons of words spelled wrong, but it said what I wanted it to say.

"Now sign and seal. Let's go drop it off."

We went to the house that night when I knew my Dad would be out with Big Lips. I taped the letter to the TV screen. That way he wouldn't miss it.

"Mission accomplished?" Lisa asked when I got back outside.

"Mission accomplished. Do you think it'll work?"

"Well, if it doesn't, we gave it our best shot."

We went back to Lisa's house for milk and cookies. Yup, we really had milk and cookies for a bedtime snack. Her mom and dad, Abby and Henry, were home from a day of hiking. Henry was a head shorter than Abby, who was this tall, beautiful blond lady. They were super nice.

After that I went to bed on the old couch in the Park's rec room and had the best night's sleep I'd had in years.

chapter eleven

The next day was Sunday. Lisa's dad made blueberry pancakes and bacon for breakfast. I didn't usually eat food that good. Then it was time for me to head home. Lisa kept asking if I had butterflies. It felt more like two heavyweight boxers duking it out in my gut.

I expected a fight when I walked in the door. My dad's never been much of a fighter though. I remembered the fights that some of my buddies had with their fathers. Cam's dad used to scream and swear at him, and Cam would scream and swear back.

Sometimes I wished my dad would yell at me. Then it might mean that he cared.

The window I broke two days before was all patched up. The house had been tidied. There was a note for me on the kitchen table: *Home at 5. Let's talk.*

Dad walked in right on the dot of five. Already I was surprised. Usually he was held up for one reason or another.

"Hi, Mike." He gave my back a firm pat. That was new too.

Dad shuffled through his CDs. He put one into our old, battered boom box. Then he sat down in his easy chair.

Kenny Rogers. "The Gambler." I loved his smoky old cowboy voice.

"Your mom and I used to sing this to you when you were a baby. When you couldn't get to sleep." He told me that every time he played the song, which wasn't often.

"I don't remember her," I said. "Mom." I told him that every time too.

My dad nodded. "You were only four when she died. Your grandma took care of you for a while, but then she died too."

"I remember Grandma. But not Mom." I'd seen photos of my mother. I knew that she had long blond hair and was pretty. I guess I got my looks from my dad.

We sat there listening. Then Dad started singing along. He had a smoky old cowboy voice too. "You gotta know when to hold 'em, know when to fold 'em. Know when to walk away, know when to run."

Dad was crying. His eyes were all crumpled up, and his moustache was catching his tears. As soon as I saw that, I started crying too.

There we were, two guys crying over Kenny Rogers.

We didn't say anything for a while, just sat there snorting and snotting all over the place. I grabbed a stack of Dairy Queen napkins from the top of the TV.

"Have you seen Kenny lately?" I said after a few minutes, my nose all plugged up. "Way too much Botox."

"Maybe a facelift too. His skin is tight as a hospital sheet," Dad said. He coughed out a chuckle.

"Yeah. Scary."

We sat there for another little while. Now Kenny was singing about Ruby not taking her love to town.

Dad cleared his throat. He pulled the letter out of his shirt pocket and unfolded it. It looked like he'd already read it a few times. "Seems you've been having a good time with all those save-the-world kids."

"Yup."

"Did you write this letter yourself?"

"Yeah. Of course." I felt my shoulders tense up.

"Fine letter there, Mike. Made me think." My shoulders relaxed a little. "You know, I really didn't think you could do it."

Dad paused, looking at the letter.

"And you saved a girl's life, you say." He looked up at me. He wanted the story.

So I told him—in great detail. I changed a few parts, but it was pretty much true.

"Sounds like you really stepped up to the plate there, Mikey."

"I guess I did."

Dad pulled the photo out of his pocket. He carefully placed it on the living-room table. "Look at all those happy little faces."

I pointed at Tim and Lisa. "That's Tim and that's Lisa. They're my two best friends at school."

"That girl's a real looker," Dad said, pointing at Lisa. "You got anything going with her?" He elbowed me in the ribs and wiggled his eyebrows up and down.

"No. Lisa's the best. She's going to be a doctor after high school. And she's a volleyball star and good at pretty much everything."

Dad just looked at me, not sure whether to nod or to shake his head. He was probably surprised to see me talking so much.

"I think I might want to go to college after high school too. And maybe I'll try out for the track team next year."

"Really? You never–" My dad stopped himself and cleared his throat. "So you're going to be a regular productive member of society. Not like your old man."

"Yeah." What was I going to do, disagree with him?

"You know, Mikey, I always thought we were a team. You and me. Like father, like son."

"Dad, if I don't stay in Explore, I'm headed straight for juvie, remember?"

"I told you we'd work that out. We have our ways, us Longridge boys."

I shook my head and stared right into his eyes. "I'm staying."

We sat there staring at each other for a minute. Dad broke the stare first.

"Want some dinner?" he asked as he jumped up out of his chair. "I, uh, bought some stuff today. Spaghetti and meatballs."

He had bought ground beef, onions and everything to make meatballs from scratch. Dad used to make meatballs when I was little. I remember helping him, squishing the meat through my fingers. I loved that feeling.

Later we settled down again, plates on our laps. We chewed in silence for a few minutes.

"So, what are we going to do, Dad?"

"I don't know, Mike. I don't know. But I can't very well stay here."

We talked for a while, trying to sort things out. We sat there, me on the couch and him in his easy chair, twirling and slurping our spaghetti until the sun set and we were sitting in darkness.

chapter twelve

So that's it. I'm staying.

My dad's leaving though. He's off to Nelson to work in a pub at a bowling alley. He leaves next week, before Christmas.

After some meetings with Officer Lando and a social worker named Barb, we got it all figured out. They decided that I should stay here and stick out the school year, since Explore is going well for me. Then we'd figure it out from there.

Lisa's parents said I could stay with them. I'm going to be in Lisa's older brother's room while he's at university. I'm so stoked.

Today was the last day of outdoor Explore, before we start regular classes in January. Five months of intense classes. I'm pretty freaked.

Rick and Maggie hosted a little awards ceremony in the afternoon. I got "Most Improved." That's got to be the worst award ever invented. It means that I really, really sucked to begin with, but hey, at least I got better. "Best Telemark Skier" or "Most Heroic" would have been better. At least part of the award was a $200 gift certificate for the local outdoor equipment store. That was pretty sweet. I think I'll put it toward some ski gear.

Next winter I'm going to learn first aid and volunteer for Ski Patrol up on the hill. Weird as it sounds, I really got a rush out of helping Kayla.

Speaking of Kayla, I think she thanked me in her own Kayla-ish way the other day.

"Was I mumbling incoherently when you found me?" she asked the Monday after we got back from the ski trip. Her arm was in a sling.

"A little," I said. Kayla narrowed her eyes. "I mean no, not really."

"Awesome, pal." She grinned and punched me in the chest with her good arm. "You're coming to the party on Friday, right?"

I wouldn't have missed it for the world.

We had a big bush party up in the hills, despite the fact that it must have been minus-twenty outside. That didn't stop the Explorers though. Tim and I lit a fire in a barrel and set off some Roman candles. Jen broke out the marshmallows, and we roasted a bunch over the barrel fire.

"You know, Mike," Tim said, "I think that without you, Explore wouldn't have been as much fun. Seriously."

"Hey, guys." It was Lisa.

"Hey," Tim and Jen said. They ran off with their burned marshmallows.

"Aren't the stars so clear out here?" Lisa asked. I looked up. They were almost as bright as that night up on the mountain.

We stood there for a while. "You worried about classes next month?" she asked.

"Totally."

"There's a class called Reading, Writing and Running."

"Seriously?"

"Yeah, it's like a modified version of English. Apparently we act out *Hamlet* some days and run five miles other days."

I smiled. Lisa smiled back. She knew what I was thinking.

Everything was going to be just fine.

Maybe.

Acknowledgments

A special thank-you to Janis McKenzie, Pat Maher, Maryn Brown and Laura Dodwell-Groves, my dear friends in writing and in life.

Christy Goerzen has been telling stories since the age of two. Her poetry and fiction has been published in various periodicals. *Explore* is her first novel. Christy lives in Vancouver, British Columbia, with her husband and two cats.

16.95   10/27/09

LONGWOOD PUBLIC LIBRARY
800 Middle Country Road
Middle Island, NY 11953
(631) 924-6400
mylpl.net

LIBRARY HOURS

Monday-Friday	9:30 a.m. - 9:00 p.m.
Saturday	9:30 a.m. - 5:00 p.m.
Sunday (Sept-June)	1:00 p.m. - 5:00 p.m.